ADAPTED BY **Gina Gold**
BASED ON THE EPISODE "NEVER JUDGE A HYENA BY ITS SPOTS," WRITTEN BY **Kevin Hopps**
FOR THE SERIES DEVELOPED FOR TELEVISION BY **Ford Riley**
ILLUSTRATED BY **Premise Entertainment**

ABDOPUBLISHING.COM

Reinforced library bound edition published in 2019 by Spotlight, a division of ABDO, PO Box 398166, Minneapolis, Minnesota 55439. Spotlight produces high-quality reinforced library bound editions for schools and libraries. Published by agreement with Disney Press, an imprint of Disney Book Group.

Printed in the United States of America, North Mankato, Minnesota.
042018   092018

DISNEY PRESS
New York • Los Angeles

THIS BOOK CONTAINS
RECYCLED MATERIALS

Library of Congress Control Number: 2017960981

Publisher's Cataloging in Publication Data

Names: Gold, Gina, author. | Hopps, Kevin, author. | Premise Entertainment, illustrator.
Title: The Lion Guard: Unlikely friends / by Gina Gold and Kevin Hopps; illustrated by Premise Entertainment.
Description: Minneapolis, MN : Spotlight, 2019 | Series: World of reading level pre-1
Summary: Kion gets lost in the Outlands when he's separated from the rest of the Lion Guard. He makes a new friend and learns an important lesson in hyena territory.
Identifiers: ISBN 9781532141812 (lib. bdg.)
Subjects: LCSH: Disney The lion guard (Television program)--Juvenile fiction. | Hyenas--Juvenile fiction. | Lion--Juvenile fiction. | Friendship--Juvenile fiction. | Readers (Primary)--Juvenile fiction.
Classification: DDC [E]--dc23

Spotlight
A Division of ABDO
abdopublishing.com

Hyenas are chasing the animals!

"Go back to the Outlands!" Kion cries.

Kion goes after Janja's crew.
The river moves fast.

Splash! Kion falls in!

Beshte and Bunga try to help.
"We're coming!" says Fuli.

"Rocks ahead!" Ono calls.

Kion swims to shore.

"I'm okay," Kion says.
"Uh-oh. This is the Outlands!"
Ono says.

Kion can't cross here.

"Meet me at Flat Ridge Rock," he says.

Bunga and his friends are lost!
"Where is Flat Ridge Rock?" Bunga asks.
The mongoose does not know.

The rhino does not know.

"There's Flat Ridge Rock!" Ono says.

11

Kion finds a trail.
Someone is watching him.

"My name is Jasiri. I can help you get to Flat Ridge Rock," the hyena says.

Kion does not listen.
He does not trust hyenas.
"That's the wrong way," says Jasiri.

"Whoaaa!" cries Kion.

Kion falls . . .

and falls.

Crunch! Kion is stuck.

"I gotcha now!" says Jasiri.

"Leave me alone!" says Kion.
"I'm freeing you, silly," says Jasiri.

"Hyenas don't help lions," says Kion.

"Not all hyenas are bad," Jasiri says.

"You're nice," Kion says.
"So are you," says Jasiri.

"We're not so different!" Jasiri says.

Jasiri sees Kion is hurt.
"I'll go with you," she says.

"There's Flat Ridge Rock," Jasiri says.

Kion thanks Jasiri.

"Good-bye, my friend," Kion says.

Kion sniffs the air . . .

"I smell Janja!" he says.

Jasiri is in trouble!

How will she get away?

Kion roars!
The clouds roar with him.

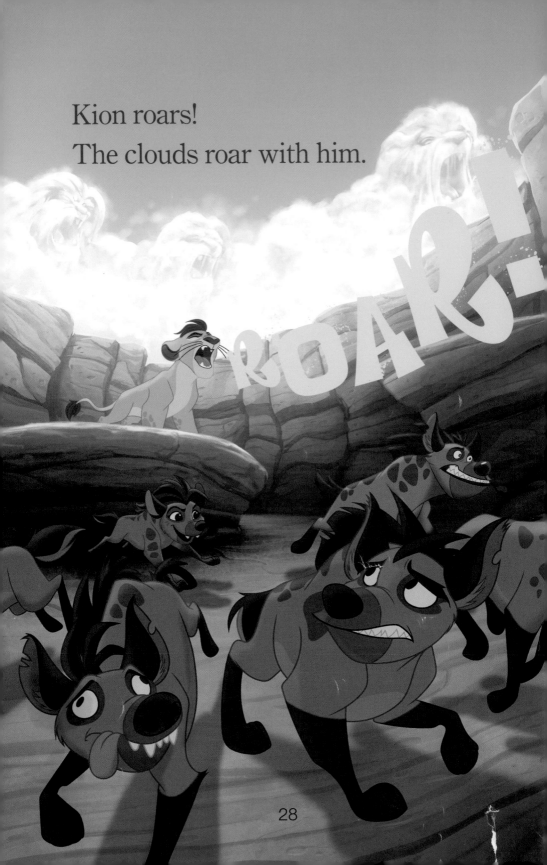

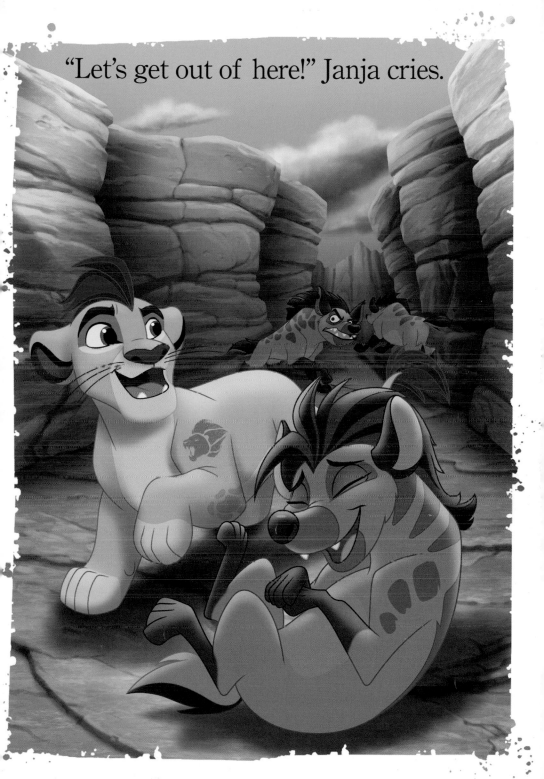

"Let's get out of here!" Janja cries.

The Lion Guard is together.
They think Kion is in trouble.
"Back off, hyena!" says Fuli.

"No! She helped me. She's my friend,"
Kion says.

"Then she's our friend, too," says Beshte. They all tell Jasiri good-bye. Kion hopes to see her soon.